Billy Bully Frog

Learns to Love

Written by **Lizzie McInerney**

Illustrated by **Jeehyun Hoke**

Winged Messengers
Clayton, North Carolina

To my family—I'm grateful for your love; it's that simple.

Bernie Beaver was named for my late brother Bernard; this is a
gift Bernie would have shared with his grandchildren.

To my cherished friends near and far—your support helped me get
to the finish line. Many thanks. We're forever bonded!

To my former kindergarten student Bekah and photographer, thank you.

Joe, it's your kindness that helps me to achieve what is needed. Jee, it's your artistic
vision that brings the story to life. You are both generous and creative gems to me.

Not all Billys are bullies. I know the sweetest Billy with leadership
qualities who always leaves an imprint on our hearts.

E. M.

Billy Bully Frog Learns to Love

Copyright © 2022 Elizabeth McInerney

Illustrations © 2022 Jeehyun Hoke

Published by Winged Messengers
Clayton, North Carolina

Book Design by Joe Eckstein, Imagine!® Studios
www.ArtsImagine.com

Edited by Beth Lottig, My Writers' Connection

ISBN: 979-8-218-04416-9
Library of Congress Control Number: 2022943572

First Winged Messengers printing: August 2022

This story is dedicated to all who have ever been bullied.
With the support of your family and friends, you can
overcome being bullied through courage and strength.
Remember to show kindness to others but,
most importantly, toward yourself.

It helps to talk to an adult you trust.
Stand up for your friends and others you see being bullied.

Bullies come in all shapes and sizes.
BULLYING is not OK!

Life at the pond has several shades of green with a splash of crystal blue. It's a beautiful, safe place to call home for all who live there.

Living in harmony delights our pond friends.

Kindness is often given and received. If a kindness reminder is needed, our pond friends know that Flory Frog will be there to help.

Flory has a special way when it comes to saying thoughtful words. One look from her big bright eyes, and you immediately feel her kindness.

Bernie Beaver is always busy, working hard to maintain the dam that keeps the pond full. It's just one way he takes care of all his pond friends.

Today, Bernie is meeting with Monty Mosquito at
Swamp Park. Monty can be a real pest when he wants to,
with his high-pitched whine and itchy bite.

But this time, he wants to ask Bernie Beaver for help.

Monty Mosquito gives Bernie Beaver the *buzzzz* about Billy Bully Frog, his friend in the swamp.

Billy is kind of a bully. He often says cruel, hurtful things. His eyes bulge, and he croaks very LOUDLY! It can be so scary!

Monty is confident that Billy Bully Frog can learn the meaning of kindness at the pond.

Bernie agrees. He whistles to gather all his pond friends.

"Billy Bully Frog will join us at the pond today," says Bernie. "He is a giant green frog with big bumps and extra-large humps. He's having a hard time and may say cruel things. He will need to feel our patience, kindness, and love."

All the pond friends agree to welcome Billy Bully Frog with kindness. Toby Turtle is tucked in his shell doing his daily meditation under the willow tree when Billy arrives.

When Toby feels Billy approach, he sticks his neck out and says, "Hello! You must be Billy Bully Frog! Welcome to the pond!"

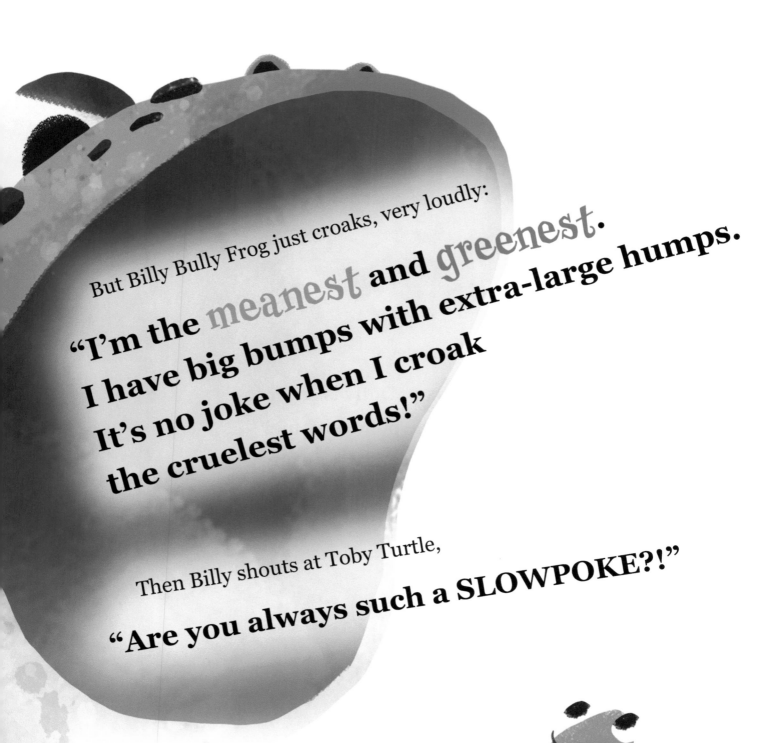

But Billy Bully Frog just croaks, very loudly:

"I'm the **meanest** and greenest.
I have big bumps with extra-large humps.
It's no joke when I croak
the cruelest words!"

Then Billy shouts at Toby Turtle,

"Are you always such a SLOWPOKE?!"

In a calm, kind voice, Toby Turtle replies, "Yes, that's who I am. I actually like that I move slowly because it gives me time to see all the beauty around me here at the pond!"

Just then, Duffy Dog runs up. Duffy is eager to play. "Billy, come run around the pond with me! It's so much fun!" he barks. "We can pick up any trash we see along the way!"

Billy Bully Frog just makes a mean face and croaks:

"I'm the meanest and greenest.
I have big bumps with extra-large humps.
It's no joke when I croak
the cruelest words!"

Billy asks,

"Are you always this happy?
I'm definitely not going to pick
up any trash. But maybe I'll
leave some. Ha ha!"

Duffy Dog tells Billy in a kind voice, "Most days,
I'm very happy. Keeping the pond crystal clear and
clean is very important to all my pond friends!"

Next, Billy finds Dolly Duck singing with her six ducklings on the pond. Dolly is so pleased. Her ducklings are very cute when they sing. Dolly Duck and her ducklings greet Billy. He hears six little voices say, "Hi, Billy!"

Billy says in his loudest, meanest croak:

"I'm the **meanest** and *greenest*.
I have big bumps with
extra-large humps.
It's no joke when I croak
the cruelest words!"

"Oh my," says Dolly Duck. "My babies don't need to hear mean words."

"Well, then we are even," says Billy with a green, bumpy sneer. **"Because I don't need to hear their singing, either!"**

Dolly Duck reminds herself to show kindness. "It might be time for you to meet Flory Frog," she says with a gentle smile.

Just then, Flory Frog swims ashore. She invites Billy Bully Frog to join her on her lily pad to catch flies together.

For the first time, Billy Bully Frog is lost for words. She's a frog, just like him!

"Billy," she says with a gentle smile, "look at your reflection in the water. What do you see?"

Billy looks down and sees an angry bully who is mean and ugly. "Being mean to others makes me think less about my big bumps with extra-large humps," he croaks—quietly this time.

Being a frog herself, Flory thinks he's very handsome and capable of kindness.

"Billy," she says, "I like your big bumps with extra-large humps. You are welcome to catch flies with me anytime!"

Flory Frog then explains to Billy how his harsh words can hurt her pond friends' feelings.

"Toby Turtle is slow because turtles are slow."

"Duffy is a dog. Dogs love to run and pick up trash."

"Dolly Duck loves her little ducklings and their sweet singing."

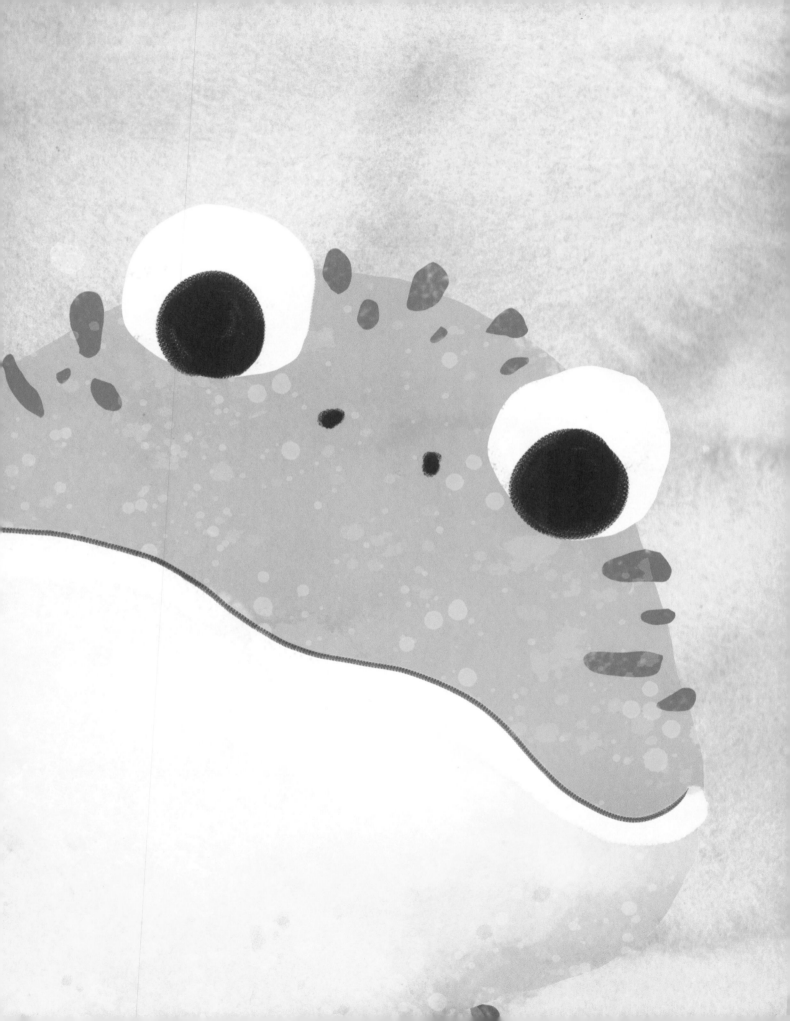

Just then, Bernie Beaver's familiar whistle interrupts them.
Once again, the pond friends stop what they are doing and listen.
"I need everyone's attention," Bernie says. "Billy, do you
have something to say?"

Billy Bully Frog now knows it's wrong to be mean. He faces the pond friends and says, "I'm very sorry for saying cruel words to you. I didn't mean to hurt your feelings.

"I realize now that it's wrong to tease and bully others. I want to be a part of this beautiful pond. I'm ready to change my anger to kindness.

"From now on, I am NOT Billy Bully Frog. I am Billy Bullfrog!"

All the pond friends smile. The ducklings sing out with their high, quacky voices:

"Billy is the sweetest and the greenest.
Billy has big, beautiful bumps with extra-large humps.
It's no joke when he croaks the kindest words!"

Billy Bullfrog is so grateful. He says, "Flory Frog and all the pond friends, thank you for showing me patience, kindness, and especially love."

"It's no joke when I croak! I'm Billy the Handsome Bullfrog— the newest pond friend!"

About the Author

Lizzie McInerney is a retired elementary school teacher with a specialization in early childhood education. Teaching young people has always been a passion of hers and writing children's books with a meaningful message is a natural extension of that passion. *Billy Bully Frog Learns to Love* is Lizzie's second book; her first, *Bella Bat Finds Her Way*, tells the heartwarming story of Bella overcoming a fear of flying with the help of her friends. The mother of two grown daughters, Lizzie resides in North Carolina with her husband of forty-two years, Terry.

About the Illustrator

Jeehyun Hoke was always one for those artistic kids. Her love for art turned into the passion for children's books, while she was in college. After studying illustration, she has illustrated various books including *Bella Bat Finds Her Way*, *Beaver's Cave Expedition*, *Goldilocks Is Back*, *Boy and the Little Violet Flower*, a coloring book, *Kick the Sparks*, and more. When she's not illustrating, she's juggling her kids' stuff as a mom.